JUSTINE McKEEN
THERMOSTAT CHAT

JUSTINE McKEEN
THERMOSTAT CHAT

Sigmund Brouwer

illustrated by Dave Whamond

orca Echoes

ORCA BOOK PUBLISHERS

Library and Archives Canada Cataloguing in Publication

Brouwer, Sigmund, 1959–, author
Justine McKeen, thermostat chat / Sigmund Brouwer ; illustrated by Dave Whamond.
(Orca echoes)

Issued in print and electronic formats.
ISBN 978-1-4598-1201-7 (paperback).—ISBN 978-1-4598-1202-4 (pdf).—
ISBN 978-1-4598-1203-1 (epub)

I. Whamond, Dave, illustrator II. Title. III. Series: Orca echoes
PS8553.R684467J87 2017   jc813'.54   c2016-904567-6
c2016-904568-4

First published in the United States, 2017
Library of Congress Control Number: 2016950083

Summary: In this illustrated early chapter book, the eighth installment in
the Justine McKeen series, Justine works with Principal Proctor to
reduce the school's energy use and save trees in the rainforest.

Orca Book Publishers gratefully acknowledges the support for its publishing programs
provided by the following agencies: the Government of Canada through the Canada Book Fund
and the Canada Council for the Arts, and the Province of British Columbia
through the BC Arts Council and the Book Publishing Tax Credit.

*Orca Book Publishers is dedicated to preserving the environment and has printed
this book on Forest Stewardship Council® certified paper.*

Cover artwork and interior illustrations by Dave Whamond
Author photo by Reba Baskett

ORCA BOOK PUBLISHERS
www.orcabook.com

Printed and bound in Canada.

20 19 18 17 • 4 3 2 1

For Savannah—your ideas are always the best! And to Orca Book Publishers, thanks for giving Justine a voice to help students help the environment!

CHAPTER ONE

"Good evening. You must be Grandpa Jim," Justine McKeen said. "Gram and I are here to get rid of vampires."

Justine and her grandmother stood on Jimmy Blatzo's front porch. Grandpa Jim had flicked on the outside light just before he opened the front door.

"It's three in the morning," Grandpa Jim croaked.

Grandpa Jim wore a bathrobe and slippers. He had a gray beard and gray hair that stuck out at all angles. He rubbed his eyes.

"This is the best time to look for vampires," Justine said.

"I'm sorry if we woke you." Gram said. "My granddaughter said your grandson was expecting us tonight."

Gram wore a flowered dress. Her hair was gray too.

"Expecting you?" Grandpa Jim said. "Did I mention it's three in the morning?"

"I don't mean to be rude," Justine said, "but if you leave the door open, the house is going to lose heat. That takes energy to replace."

Justine took her gram's hand, walked them both inside and shut the door behind her.

Grandpa Jim looked at the closed door. He looked at Justine.

"Well, I don't mean to be rude," Grandpa Jim said. "But who are you?"

"This is my gram and my name is Justine," Justine said. She grabbed Grandpa Jim's hand and shook it up and down. "How about we shut off the outside light?"

Justine pulled a small notebook out of her back pocket. She flipped it open. She pulled a short pencil from her front pocket. She made a small mark in the notebook. She flipped it shut. She put the notebook in her back pocket and the pencil in her front pocket.

"I'm Doreen," Gram said to Grandpa Jim with a smile. "And again, I apologize. Justine said Jimmy insisted that we come over at this time of night. And I wasn't going to let Justine walk here alone. I'm her legal guardian."

Grandpa Jim rubbed his eyes again. "Justine McKeen, the Queen of Green? Jimmy left a note on his bedroom door about you."

"See, Gram?" Justine said. "I told you Jimmy expected us."

"The note did not say anything about waking me up at three in the morning," Grandpa Jim said. "Or anything about vampires."

"I knocked on the door as loud as I could," Justine explained. "I thought that would get Jimmy out of bed."

"You *were* very loud," Grandpa Jim said. "I should point out there is a doorbell."

"Gram and I disconnected our doorbell," Justine said. "Anything to get rid of vampires."

"Vampires don't like doorbells?" asked Grandpa Jim.

"Doorbells *are* vampires."

Grandpa Jim reached over and pinched Justine's shoulder.

"Ouch!"

"Huh," Grandpa Jim said. "You *are* real. I thought maybe my new medications were too strong."

"I have that same problem," Gram said to Grandpa Jim. "By the way, that's a nice bathrobe. Did your wife get it for you?"

"I'm a widower," Grandpa Jim said. "I'm here for a couple of weeks while Jimmy's parents are out of town."

"Your girlfriend then," Gram said. "She has good taste in bathrobes."

"No girlfriend either," Grandpa Jim said. He slicked back his messy hair with his hands.

He smiled at Gram.

Gram smiled at him.

"Since you're here anyway," Grandpa Jim told Gram, "would you like me to make you a cup of tea?"

"No time for idle chat," Justine said. "We'll make sure your thermostat is turned down. It's the first and easiest way to stop vampires. Then let's wake up Jimmy and track down the rest of those vampires."

CHAPTER TWO

The three of them stood outside Jimmy's bedroom door. A note was tacked to it.

"Mules are very smart," Justine said. "I'll have to thank Jimmy for this nice note."

"What's that noise?" Grandpa Jim asked. It was coming from the other side of the door.

"It sounds like a Justin Bieber song," Gram said.

"What is a Justin Bieber?" Grandpa Jim asked.

Gram patted Grandpa Jim's hand. "You are better off to never know. Now how about that tea?"

Grandpa Jim smiled at Gram.

Gram smiled at Grandpa Jim.

Justine knocked on the door.

"Good luck," Grandpa Jim said. "It takes a lot more than a loud song to wake him during the night. He's always been like this."

Grandpa Jim opened the door and turned on the bedroom light.

Jimmy's radio alarm blared.

"Please," Grandpa Jim begged. "Make it stop."

Justine stepped across the bedroom and turned off the alarm. Jimmy was deep in sleep on his back. He was wearing pajamas with a puppy-dog pattern, and a puppy-dog hoodie. He had his arm around a stuffed bear, and he was snoring. There was a shiny line of drool from his lips down his cheeks to his pillow.

"Hey, Blatzo," Justine whispered.

Jimmy kept snoring.

"Blatzo!"

Jimmy kept snoring.

"Well," Justine said to Gram and Grandpa Jim, "now I understand why

he hasn't tracked down the vampires like he promised."

"About these vampires," Grandpa Jim said. "I would really like to know what's going on."

"Since Jimmy won't wake up," Justine answered, "maybe instead you can take me around the house to track them down. We'll start with your thermostat."

"I'm so confused," Grandpa Jim said.

"I often feel that way around Justine," Gram said. "She does a lot more talking than listening. Tea?"

"Yes, please," Grandpa Jim said.

"Vampires first," Justine insisted. "Well, not quite first. I'm sure glad I have my iPod with me."

CHAPTER THREE

"My plan is that we get all the kids in the school to think of them as vampires lurking around in the dark," Justine told the school's new principal, Dr. Proctor. "Then we'll hunt them."

Justine had come to school early to meet Dr. Proctor in his office. He was a big man with a big belly and big teeth and a big mustache over those big teeth.

As usual, he wore a suit with a vest. The vest stretched over his belly.

He sat behind his desk.

Justine stood in front of his desk.

"Vampires?" he said.

"They suck energy just like vampires suck blood," she said. "A little here and a little there. After a while, a lot is missing."

"Mosquitos do the same thing," Dr. Proctor said. "Except for after, when your skin itches. Do vampire bites do that?"

"I don't think that's the point," Justine said. Sometimes she missed the principal who had been at the school before Dr. Proctor. "If we are going to put up posters in the school to look for things that drain electricity, what sounds more exciting? Hunting for vampires, or hunting for mosquitos? I can tell you that last night Jimmy Blatzo's grandfather sure paid attention when I told him we needed to find all the vampires in the house."

"Mosquitos are real," Dr. Proctor said. "Vampires are not. If it's true that these things cost our school so much energy, shouldn't we name them after something real?"

"Dr. Proctor, a poster that tells students to squish the energy mosquitos won't have the same kind of impact as this one."

Justine unrolled a poster that she had designed and drawn. It said SLAY THE ENERGY VAMPIRES. She had used lots of red felt pen, and it showed big fangs and dripping blood.

Dr. Proctor twirled the ends of his mustache in his fingers. Justine noticed he did that when he was thinking about something. Just like a few weeks ago when she had finally convinced him to go along with her new plan to save energy at the school.

"You are right about the poster getting attention," Dr. Proctor finally said. "Even so, there is a problem with this. We have small children at the school. Many of them won't understand that we are trying to get them to help keep track of things that drain energy. They might worry that the vampire is real and in the school."

It didn't take Justine very long to decide that Dr. Proctor was correct. "You're right. It would be wrong to frighten little kids."

Justine folded the poster. She walked over to Dr. Proctor's blue bin in the corner of the office and put the paper there. She pulled an envelope out of her backpack. From the envelope she took out a small sticker of a tree.

There were also times Justine was glad Dr. Proctor was the new principal.

"For you," Justine said, handing it to Dr. Proctor. "I've taken note of all you do in your office to help the environment. Your blinds are open, so you can keep your lights off. Your computer is shut off when you leave at the end of the day. You have the blue bin to recycle. And your lunch bag is reusable. Over the course of a year, all of this adds up to one tree saved in the rainforest." She handed the tree sticker to Dr. Proctor.

"Thank you," Dr. Proctor said. "Now, what about some other ideas for your poster?"

"How about one that has lots and lots of dollar bills drawn on it? People get excited about money."

"That's a great idea," Dr. Proctor said. "After all, the reason I ordered those energy-detecting devices for the

school was because you showed me how much money we could save. The device shows how much electricity you are using minute by minute, and it sends the information to an app or a website. If we monitor our use and learn how and where to cut back on electricity, we can save tens of thousands of dollars a year. And that's nothing to sneeze at."

"You just came up with a great idea for a poster!"

"You mean a picture of a nose that sneezes out money instead of..."

"Not that," Justine said. "My new poster could have a famous detective on it. It could say *Become like Sherlock Holmes and find energy thieves.*"

"Much better," Dr. Proctor said. "So who is going to help you in your detective work after school today?"

"Jimmy Blatzo," Justine said.

"Jimmy Blatzo?" Dr. Proctor said. "I'm surprised. He doesn't like doing stuff like this."

"Trust me," Justine said. "After I have lunch with him today, he'd wear a clown outfit to school if I told him it needed to be done."

CHAPTER FOUR

Justine sat with Jimmy Blatzo at a table in the cafeteria. Their friend Safdar walked up to them.

"Give me five," Safdar said, holding up a palm for Justine.

She slapped. Then she touched her own palm. "Ewww."

Safdar giggled. "Great trick, huh? I smeared it with petroleum jelly. It's clear and feels yucky. I can hardly wait to do it to Michael."

"Would you mind getting me a napkin?" she asked him.

"Then why bother playing the trick?" Safdar said.

"How about you get her a napkin," Jimmy Blatzo said to Safdar.

"Sure," Safdar said. "I'll be right back."

"Thanks, Blatzo," Justine said.

"Don't call me Blatzo," he said.

"Of course," she answered. "Blatzo, it would be great if you helped me with something after school. It's for the environment."

"Um, no," he said. "I'm already helping at home. My gramps said you stopped by last night and shut down all the energy vampires. I had set my alarm to help you, but I slept through it."

"You also slept through me visiting your room," Justine said.

Before he could answer, their friend Michael reached the table.

"Hey, Justine," Michael said. "Here's a straw."

"I try not to use straws," Justine said. "But since it will go to waste if I don't, thank you."

She put the straw in her milk and began to sip. Drops of milk dribbled down the front of her shirt.

Michael giggled. "Great trick, huh? I poked the straw full of pin holes. I can hardly wait to do it to Safdar."

"Would you mind getting me a napkin?" she asked.

"Then why bother playing the trick?" Michael said.

"How about you get her a napkin," Jimmy Blatzo said to Michael.

"Sure," Michael said. "I'll be right back."

That left just the two of them again.

"After school, I need your help going through the building and looking for MELS," Justine said to Jimmy. "Just like we're doing at your house."

"I don't know what a MEL is, and I am not the volunteering type of guy," Blatzo said. "You know that. And usually when I help you, something goes wrong. I'm still amazed that nothing bad happened last night."

"Don't be too sure about that," Justine said. She grabbed some chewing gum from her backpack and put it in her mouth.

As she chewed, she found her iPod. She tapped the screen.

"You'll want to help me after seeing this," she said to Jimmy. She held out the iPod. "I took this photo during my visit last night, while you were asleep."

Jimmy's face turned white when he saw the screen. He tried to take the iPod, but Justine pulled it away. That's when Michael and Safdar returned.

"Give me five," Safdar said to Michael.

"Sure," Michael said. "And here's a straw for you."

Safdar took the straw. Michael gave Safdar a high five.

"Ewww," Michael said. He shook his hand. "What's this gross stuff?"

Safdar giggled. He put the straw in his juice and sucked. Juice dribbled down his shirt. Michael giggled.

"Might as well go and get each other napkins," Justine said. "When you come back, Blatzo and I are going to tell you how you can both become detectives."

"Cool," Michael said.

"Cool," Safdar said.

As they walked away, Justine pulled the chewing gum out of her mouth. She stretched it into two pieces. She put one piece on the seat of Michael's chair. She put the second piece on the seat of Safdar's chair.

"Really," she said. "You'd think they'd learn by now, wouldn't you?"

"Me too," Jimmy said. His face was still white with fear from seeing the photo on the iPod. "You'd think I'd also have learned by now."

CHAPTER FIVE

After Michael and Safdar sat at the table, Justine spoke to both of them.

"After school, the two of you are going to help me and Blatzo hunt for MELS."

"We are?" Michael asked.

"You are," Jimmy said.

"Of course we are," Michael said. "Right, Safdar?"

"What's a MEL?" Safdar asked. "Nothing dangerous, right? I'm not a big fan of danger."

"Go ahead, Blatzo," Justine said. "I'll let you explain."

"No thanks," he said. "I'm not the Queen of Green."

"Hmm," Justine said. "Where exactly did I put my iPod and the photo on it?"

"MEL is short for miscellaneous electric load," Jimmy quickly said.

"Miss what?" Michael said.

Jimmy sighed. "Miss. Ull. Lane. Eee. Us. That means a bunch of something. In this case, a bunch of things that are constantly drawing small amounts of electricity when we aren't using them."

"Miscellaneous electric load," Safdar said. "I knew that."

Jimmy said, "Sure. You knew they were things like computers and microwaves and doorbells and home-entertainment centers and printers and stuff like that."

"Keep going," Justine said to Jimmy. "I'm proud of you."

"MELS can use up to fifteen percent of an energy bill," Jimmy said. "For a school like ours, that can be twenty thousand dollars a year. And if every school and home cut down on MELS, it would be huge in the fight against man-made global warming."

"You sound better than me," Justine told Jimmy. "And would you mind telling us how we can measure MELS?"

Jimmy sighed again. "You put a gadget called a home energy monitor

on your home or school electric meter. It sends information to a program that you can watch on a website. The best time to check for MELs is when you know big appliances that draw a lot of energy, like your air-conditioning unit, aren't being used. Also, you have to be sure to check your thermostat all the time so that you don't waste energy heating or cooling the house when it doesn't need it."

"Yes," Justine said. "At home, the best time is around three in the morning, when nothing else is drawing electricity. Jimmy agreed to measure MELs at his house. So we measured his home's usual electricity use for five nights in a row. Last night we disconnected all his MELs at that hour, like the DVD player and computer and cable box on his television, and measured how much it cut down on electricity compared to the previous days. Twelve percent!"

Justine leaned forward. "Dr. Proctor also has an energy monitor set up at the school. We now have five days' worth of usage to know what the average is. After school today, the four of us are going to go from classroom to classroom and shut down everything with a MEL. Then we'll compare the school's electricity use to the average and see how much energy we saved."

"Sounds like fun," Michael said. "Or maybe I could scrub toilets instead."

"Listen to me very carefully," Jimmy said. He paused. "Grrrr."

"MEL detecting it is!" Michael said. "See you after school."

"Real fun," Safdar said. "I can hardly wait."

They both stood and walked away. Justine's chewing gum was stuck to the rear end of each of their pants.

"An old trick," Justine said, "but a good one, wouldn't you agree?"

"I agree that I'm helping you tonight," Jimmy said. "And you'll agree to delete the photo on your iPod?"

"But you look so sweet in your puppy-dog pajamas," Justine said. "And the hoodie is adorable."

"Stop right there, and I can explain the stuffed bear. Really."

CHAPTER SIX

"Well, Blatzo, that almost does it for our list," Justine said to Jimmy.

"Almost?" he said. "*Almost*? You already sent Michael and Safdar home. How about us?"

They were walking toward the custodian's office in a hallway at the end of the school. Jimmy pointed at a clock on the wall. "See how late it is?"

"Five PM," she said. "And notice how easy it is to see the time?"

"Five PM," he repeated.

"Every microwave and DVD player and all the other stuff in the school that has a digital clock draws electricity. And we have a clock right in front of us. We don't need to see the time on all of those other electronics. Aren't you glad we shut off all the MELS?"

Jimmy groaned. "I just want to go home."

"Almost," she said.

Justine pulled a small notebook out of her back pocket. She flipped it open. She pulled a short pencil from her front pocket. She made some small marks in the notebook. She flipped it shut. She put the notebook in her back pocket and the pencil in her front pocket.

"By my calculations," she said, "you have earned yourself a tree. As soon as we get back to my backpack, I will give you an official award from my envelope."

"A tree sticker," Jimmy said. "I can't wait."

"It's not the sticker that matters," she said. "It's what it represents. All the little things you did today add up, and over the course of a year you have reduced carbon emissions as much as if you had planted a new tree in the rainforest."

"Well," he said, "when you put it like that, then I am happy to have earned a tree sticker. But not so happy we aren't finished. What's left?"

"We need to talk to our custodian."

"Mr. Barnes? Have you ever heard some of the music he plays in his office? AC/DC and other heavy metal rock. I heard he's even in some kind of Battle of the Bands concert this weekend."

"I know," Justine said. "He has posters of heavy metal bands up on every wall in his office. If Dr. Proctor didn't tell him about our hunt for MELS, he might go around turning things back on. I've been keeping my eye out for him, but I haven't seen him in the halls."

"Weird," Jimmy said. "Usually you can't get away from him. He has eyes everywhere."

"Oh, good," Justine said. She stopped at the custodian's door. "He's back in his office."

The door was closed, and his office did not have windows.

"How do you know?" Jimmy asked.

"See under the door? His light is on. He used to forget to turn it off, but after we talked about it a few times, he learned to remember. So now the only time the light is on is when he's in his office."

Justine knocked on the door. "Mr. Barnes, it's Justine."

From behind the door, he said, "I'm not here."

"Then why is your light on?"

The light went off, and underneath the door it went dark.

"I'm not here," he said.

"Then I'll just wait until you get back," Justine said. "Right outside this door. The only way in or out of your office."

A second later the door opened. Only a little bit. Mr. Barnes stuck his head through the opening so that Justine couldn't see inside his office. The light was still off.

"Fine," Mr. Barnes said. "I'll get this over with. What crazy idea are you selling me today?"

Justine smiled. "What's on your face? You have something black under your eyes."

The door closed. The light went on. Five seconds later the door opened.

The black stuff on Mr. Barnes's face was gone.

"Yes?" Mr. Barnes said. Again, only his head showed through the opening of the door.

"We just wanted to let you know that Jimmy and I and Michael and Safdar went around the school shutting off anything that drains electricity. If you see anything we missed, would you mind unplugging it?"

"That's it?" Mr. Barnes said. "Nothing crazy like collecting dog poop or knitting sweaters from dog fur or selling plastic plates made from pig pee?"

"Not this time," Justine said. "But if I think of something, you'll be the first to know."

Mr. Barnes groaned, pulled his head back and shut his door.

CHAPTER SEVEN

"This is crazy!" Justine called out. "Gram, come and look!"

It was nine o'clock. Justine was in front of the computer that she and her gram shared.

Gram was sitting on the nearby couch. She marked the page in the book she'd been reading and walked over to the computer.

"You might have to explain to me what you think is crazy," Gram said. "I just see a bunch of lines and numbers."

"Remember how our school principal brought in two energy monitors because I promised him it would save a lot of money if we found the electricity vampires?"

"Of course I do," Gram said. "One for homes and one for schools. And didn't he agree that the school would lend out the home energy monitor to anyone who wanted to save electricity?"

"Yes, yes," Justine said. "We checked our home first. And then Jimmy Blatzo's home. The monitors send out information, and all it takes is a computer to see how much electricity is being used at any time. That's what we're looking at. It's called a *dashboard*."

The computer screen was filled with graphs and lines that moved up and down.

"It's a wonderful idea," Gram said.

"But this is strange," Justine said. "Right now we're looking at the graph for the monitor at Jimmy Blatzo's house. Remember last night how the electricity use went down after we turned off all of the MELS?"

Gram nodded.

"Right now," Justine said, "the graph shows that electricity use is way up. Almost like every light is on in the house and also the television and the washer and dryer."

Justine moved the computer mouse, and a new graph came up. "This is crazy too. Here's the school graph. After school, my friends helped me shut off all of the energy vampires. Compared to the last five nights, the school should have been using about fifteen percent less energy."

"Yes," Gram said. "That's what you promised Dr. Proctor."

"But nothing changed!" Justine said. "It just doesn't make sense."

"I'm sure you'll figure it out," Gram said. "You always come up with something."

"I wish I could go to the school right now and try to figure it out, but the school is locked."

Justine switched the computer screen back to the graph that showed the electricity use at Jimmy Blatzo's house.

"At least for Jimmy's house," Justine said, "I can give him a call and see what's happening over there."

Gram said, "Wouldn't it be better to see for yourself? You carry that notebook of yours everywhere, and what if Jimmy doesn't find everything in the house that's using electricity? Plus, he will probably be asleep, and nothing wakes him up."

"Good thinking," Justine said. "Are you sure you don't mind walking over there with me?"

Gram patted Justine's hand. "To help you help the planet, I'm happy to do my part. But would you mind waiting a few minutes? I need to fix my hair."

CHAPTER EIGHT

"This is not looking good," Jimmy Blatzo said to Justine as they strolled down an empty hallway near the front of the school.

It was nearly seven in the evening the next day, and the school was very quiet.

"You mean because Dr. Proctor is in a bad mood because he had to meet us here tonight to supervise as we wander around the school looking for MELS after hours?"

"Yup," Jimmy said.

"And because we just spent half an hour and couldn't find anything that was adding to the school's electricity load?"

"Yup," Jimmy said.

"And because Dr. Proctor is probably going to be mad that the school bought energy monitors and they're not showing we're saving him money like I promised?"

"Yup," Jimmy said.

"And because when we get to his office, we're going to have to tell him the bad news?"

"Nope," Jimmy said.

"Nope?"

"*We* aren't going to tell him the bad news. *You* are. I'm going to wait in the hallway while you go into his office. Alone."

"I'm going to have to tell him that just because sometimes it doesn't work like you wanted, it doesn't mean you shouldn't try to make things better."

As they continued to walk, Justine pulled her small notebook from her back pocket and flipped it open. "But at least we fixed stuff that can help the school become more green. Shut off a dripping tap in the art room. Replaced missing recycling bins in two classrooms. Closed four windows that had been left open after school. Add these up over the course of a year, and it's enough points to—"

"Give ourselves another tree sticker?" Jimmy said.

"Exactly."

Justine snapped her fingers. "Hey, this has given me a great idea. Maybe we could set up a daily school patrol where kids look for things that will help the environment. With this system I have, you get points for every little thing you do, and you can see how they add up. Kids could get tree stickers. Or, better yet, classrooms could get stickers and put them on a chart, and we could have a contest for the classroom that earns the most trees. And if we're going to do that, what if kids also kept track of what they did at home for more tree stickers for the contest?"

Justine put the notebook back in her pocket. "Yup," she said. "I am brilliant."

"Nope," Jimmy said.

"But—"

"What's in your other back pocket?" Jimmy asked.

"My iPod," Justine answered. "The one where I deleted the photo of you with the stuffed—"

"Your iPod," Jimmy said. "Most kids have devices but hardly any carry around little notebooks. Wouldn't it be way better to use an app to keep track of how you help the environment?"

"Wow," Justine said. "You're the one who is brilliant. Now if you could just figure out why shutting off all the school's MELS didn't cut down on the electrical load yesterday…"

Jimmy put up a hand. "Listen. What's that?"

Justine cocked her head and squinted. "I can barely hear it, but it sounds like rock music."

"AC/DC-heavy-metal kind of rock music," Jimmy said. "Maybe from the drama room down at the end of the other hallway?"

"Heavy metal rock music," Justine said. "But who would be playing rock music this loud at this time of night?"

CHAPTER NINE

Justine and Jimmy stood in the hallway outside the drama room. The music was so loud that it felt like the floor was vibrating.

Justine cracked open the door. Jimmy stood on his tiptoes and peeked over her head.

Now the music was so loud that Justine winced.

She shut the door.

"Did you see what I saw?" she whispered to Jimmy.

She realized that Jimmy couldn't hear a whisper over the music, and that there was no reason to try to be quiet.

"Did you see what I saw?" she asked.

"I'm afraid," Jimmy said. "Very afraid. Was that Mr. Barnes?"

Justine cracked open the door again.

All the floodlights in the drama room were pointed at the stage, and the rest of the room was dark, the way it was when students put on a play for parents.

Except nobody was in the audience.

Mr. Barnes was alone on the stage.

But he didn't look like the custodian Mr. Barnes. His face was fully painted with black and white makeup, just like the musicians on the posters in his office.

He wore a tight black outfit with a long cape, and he stood in front of a microphone, holding a guitar.

He played the guitar with his back arched away from the microphone and screamed out the words to the song.

Justine shut the door.

"That's a lot of music for one person," Jimmy said.

"I think he has all the speakers on and is playing along to a song," she said.

She opened the door again. They both watched.

She shut the door again.

"Yes," Justine said. "That's exactly what is happening."

"What should we do?" Jimmy asked. "Tell Dr. Proctor?"

"He looks like he is having so much fun," Justine said. "If that was you, would you want the school to know about it?"

"No," Jimmy said. "If he wanted this to be a secret, we'll keep it a secret."

"I'm glad you agree," Justine said. "He must be practicing for the Battle of the Bands contest this weekend. Which means that next week we can probably show Dr. Proctor that shutting down all the MELS actually does work."

"That makes us great energy detectives, right?"

"Except for one last thing," Justine said.

"What's that?" Jimmy asked.

"Remember the photo I took of you when you were asleep with the stuffed—"

"I do not remember any photo," Jimmy said. "And neither do you."

"Of course," Justine said. "But if I did, it would remind me that maybe we should take some video of Mr. Barnes dressed up like he is. You never know when we might be able to use it."

"That kind of thinking," Jimmy said, "is why I am frightened of you."

Justine opened the door again. This time with the iPod in her hand.

CHAPTER TEN

At home that night, using an art program on her computer, Justine finished drawing the final part of her poster and adding the words at the bottom.

BE A SHERLOCK "HOMES" DETECTIVE!

GET RID OF ENERGY THIEVES WHERE YOU LIVE!!

She was very proud of *HOMES* instead of *HOLMES*. She wondered if she had used too many exclamation points. Then she decided to add more.

BE A SHERLOCK "HOMES" DETECTIVE!!!!!

GET RID OF ENERGY THIEVES WHERE YOU LIVE!!!!!!!

Much better, she thought. Because you can never be too excited about helping keep the planet green.

"Gram," she said, "before I start to color this, do you want to see how it looks?"

Gram was sitting on the couch. She put her book down. As she walked across the room to Justine, the phone on the computer desk rang.

Justine answered it. "Hello?"

She paused. "Oh, hello, Grandpa Jim."

She paused again. "Sure, I'll take a look. I'm at the computer right now."

Justine switched programs, and the energy-monitor graph came up on her computer screen. She stared at the numbers and lines and frowned.

"You are right, Grandpa Jim," Justine said into the telephone. "Just ask Jimmy—he should be able to show you what you are doing wrong."

Justine listened to his answer. She put her hand over the mouthpiece of the telephone and spoke to Gram. "He said Jimmy's already asleep. And everyone knows you can't wake him up."

Justine listened on the phone again. Then she said to Grandpa Jim, "Sure, I'll tell her you need help."

Justine hung up the phone.

"Gram, this is crazy!" Justine said. "I thought last night that we had done a good job of explaining to Grandpa Jim how to reduce their electrical load. But the home-energy graph shows he still doesn't understand."

Gram grabbed her purse, walked over to the far wall of the living room and looked at herself in a mirror. She patted her hair, took some lipstick out of her purse and added some to her lips.

As she looked in the mirror, Gram said, "I remember everything that you told Grandpa Jim last night. How about you stay at home and work on your poster. I'll go over by myself to give him help."

"Wow, Gram," Justine said. "I'm so glad that you care about the planet."

"It is important to be green, Justine," Gram said. "I'm happy to do my part."

"You're the best, Gram," Justine said.

"I know." Gram smiled. "It may take hours to help Jimmy's grandfather. Hours and hours. So don't think you have to wait up until I get home. And maybe I'll have to go back tomorrow night if he is a slow learner."

Gram took one final look at herself in the mirror and smoothed her hair. She waved goodbye and left the house.

"Grandpa Jim is nice, but he sure is a slow learner," Justine said to herself as she began to work on her poster again. "If he doesn't figure this out soon, I might not be able to give him a tree sticker."

Sigmund Brouwer is the bestselling author of many books for children and young adults, including the popular Justine McKeen, Queen of Green series. *Justine McKeen, Thermostat Chat* is the eigth book in the series. Sigmund lives in Red Deer, Alberta and Nashville, Tennessee. For more information, visit www.rockandroll-literacy.com.